Grandpa's

Story by Carmel Reilly

Illustrations by Jenny Mountstephen

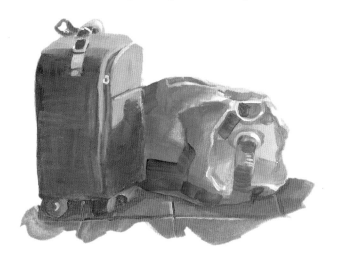

Rigby®

A Harcourt Achieve Imprint

www.Rigby.com
1-800-531-5015

Mom put the phone down.

"That was Grandpa!"

she said to Tessa and Alice.

"He is coming to stay with us

for two or three nights,

and he is on his way **now!**"

"Where will he sleep?" said Tessa.

"Grandpa can have your room, Tessa," said Mom.

"But I want Grandpa to have **my** room," said Alice.
"My bedroom is better. It's bigger."

"Yes, your bedroom **is** bigger,"
Tessa said to Alice.
"It has two beds.
So I will come and sleep
in your room,
and Grandpa can have my room."

Alice looked at Tessa's room.

"Your things are all over the floor," she said. "Grandpa can't sleep in here."

"Yes, he can," said Mom. "Come on, Alice. It's getting late. Please help us get Tessa's room ready."

They all helped.

Tessa took some of her things
into Alice's bedroom.

Mom made the bed.

Alice put Tessa's toys into a box
and moved it under the bed.

"That looks better," said Mom.

"The room is ready now."

"We **did** it," said Alice.

"Oh no!" said Tessa.

"We forgot the clean towels."

She ran to get them.

Alice looked out the window.

"Grandpa is here!" she shouted.

The girls raced outside.

"Come and see your room, Grandpa," said Tessa. "It's all ready for you."

Grandpa put his bags down.

"I'm going to like staying here,"

he smiled.